T0274545

BRIEF
LIVES

BRIEF
LIVES

BRIEF LIVES

FICTIONS

KEITH HAZZARD

EXILE
editions

SINGULAR FICTION, POETRY, NONFICTION, TRANSLATION, DRAMA, AND GRAPHIC BOOKS

2024

Library and Archives Canada Cataloguing in Publication

Title: Brief lives : fictions / Keith Hazzard.
Names: Hazzard, Keith, author.
Identifiers: Canadiana (print) 20240478436 | Canadiana (ebook) 20240481887 |
    ISBN 9781990773549 (softcover) | ISBN 9781990773570 (PDF) |
    ISBN 9781990773556 (EPUB) | ISBN 9781990773563 (Kindle)
Subjects: LCGFT: Short stories.
Classification: LCC PS8615.A99 B75 2024 | DDC C813/.6—dc23

Copyright © Keith Hazzard, 2024
Book and cover designed by Michael Callaghan
Cover and Interior artwork by Melkor3D/Shutterstock
Typeset in Garamond and Trajan Pro fonts at Moons of Jupiter Studios
Published by Exile Editions Ltd ~ www.ExileEditions.com
    144483 Southgate Road 14, Holstein, Ontario, N0G 2A0
Printed and bound in Canada by Marquis

This is a work of fiction; therefore, each story and all characters are fictitious.
Any public agencies, institutions, or historical figures mentioned in the story serve
as a backdrop to the characters and their actions, which are wholly imaginary.

Exile Editions supports copyright.

Copyright fuels creativity, encourages diverse voices, promotes free speech,
    and creates a vibrant culture. Thank you for purchasing an authorized edition
    of this book and for complying with copyright laws.

You may request written permission from the publisher (info@exileeditions.com)
    if you would like to reproduce, scan, photocopy, or distribute any part of this book;
    and/or a reproductive copying license can be obtained from Access Copyright.

Your support of writers and artists is what allows Exile Editions to continue
    to publish books for readers worldwide.

We gratefully acknowledge the Government of Canada and Ontario Creates for
    their financial support toward our publishing activities.

.We warmly thank Aetna Pest Control (Toronto) for their ongoing support.

Canadian sales representation:
The Canadian Manda Group, 664 Annette Street, Toronto ON M6S 2C8
www.mandagroup.com 416 516 0911

North American and international distribution, and U.S. sales:
Independent Publishers Group, 814 North Franklin Street,
Chicago IL 60610 www.ipgbook.com toll free: 1 800 888 4741

for Karen

I

II

III

I

EROS

Alison Dross, fresh from mortuary school, learned to ski, drink and enjoy sex, mostly with Ed Campbell, who moved on to Vail, leaving Alison lonely among her charmless friends and staid corpses. Close brick corners was the feeling. Any little thing pricking and stinging was also the feeling. And waking airless. Getting the face-cage set. The right stone on the tongue. The heavy feet turned around and pointed downhill, and rolling along, every morning, into the Underworld.

Alison was dating Jason Robb, scion of Robb Cement, and tending her retorts when Ed got in touch. He was married. Too much so, he said, and could not forget the midnight saunas, the pulse of her thigh sprinting in his ear. She flew to Aspen. Ed's marvellous chest went with her to her room, and she was amazed, in her full body, for two atavistic nights, then Ed went home to his family and bright was drear again.

That spring Alison married Andrew Simms, of Simms Flour, who had taught her how to bring her shoulder firmly through the ball. They bought bigger freezers, better urns. They expanded the rooms of mourning. Andrew deepened his oenophilia. Alison swam more laps at the club. Georgia died before she was born. For their fifth anniversary they returned to the Bahamas. Everything was the same, all around them. They drank on the beach until they were empty of argument.

Andrew bought a winery and moved upstate. Alison got the house and the silence. She took up painting, yoga, Reiki, dyed her hair auburn, started seeing Caleb Summer, whose father she had known, a difficult case craniofacially. Caleb worked in arbitrage, shaking the money tree. Some nights he wore a wig and she slapped him. Other nights they rode around in this car or that car, looking in windows. One night he yearned to be crucified.

Ed was in Vermont at that time. He sold kayaks and now everyone had one. Alison sent money. They met in motels. He was back with his wife. His daughter was in middle school. She didn't seem to like him. If he had his life to do over, he wouldn't, he said. One afternoon Alison watched him walk to his car, watched him shrink and disappear into the glass prongs of the winter rain. She was thirty-five. She stopped embalming and sold the business, a little below value. The afterlife could take care of itself.

MONDAY

Jay Brunson had a good breakfast. His mother didn't call. The truck started and the sun stayed with him all the way to work. His preferred spot was open. He backed in perfectly. There was nothing wrong with the day.

Jay had last week's paperwork to finish. Instead he took a stroll through the building. There were more doors than he remembered and the lunchroom was clean, as if only good people used it. He opened a loud package and ate a cookie.

Ann from Purchasing let him sign her cast. Then he was standing by the fire extinguisher, putting pressure drops in his eyes. Samir came along, wearing that grin. Brad was right behind, wearing the same grin. It was one of those moments that can happen only once.

The window in his office was hard to open. It always had been. He used a knife to work the catch. The little air that entered was not fresh. Jay went outside. His truck was still there, running smoothly. He could go anywhere he wanted, at any time. There are two clocks in the world, he thought, one inside the other, and it is that one, the smaller, that decides things.

TORMENTED BY CIRCUS MUSIC

Late one evening in his fortieth year, after smashing every window in the house but before setting fire to the garage, Hazen Todd, claims adjuster, explained to his wife that, no, he was not acting like an animal, he was an animal, specifically a bear, although not a prime bear with a paradise of kills to look forward to, but an old, half-blind, shuffling bear that had never in its impossible life understood its true nature, and was now so tired, obscenely tired of pretending, yet condemned, there was no other word, still condemned every day to repeat the effort to be human, which might be justifiable if you're human already but only humiliating if you're not, so surely she could see, must see if sense yet lived in her, that any further reference, including silent reference, to the chain of missteps that had led him and, yes, her as well, to this present havoc would, he was certain, bring them no comfort since the very powers now working through him were the same that had for so long, much longer than he could remember, at least forced him to his feet and put one thought in front of another but by then his wife was not listening, had not been listening or even present for many years, although the following week she did write his obituary and in it searched for the good.

INCIDENT

On the 18th of November at 23:30 Karlheinz Breuer, a 29-year-old male of no fixed address, entered the Pot of Gold Lounge on Argyle Street and made statements to the effect that:

he was raised with a true knowledge of evil and had never forgotten it but could no longer tell his right hand from his left hand and would give all he had, $12 and a lighter, to anyone who could set him straight without removing the bandages;

the $12 had been earned by honest effort;

the lighter was genuine gold;

the man beaten to death behind the bus station had nothing to do with him;

he was through searching his soul for insects.

Asked to leave, Karlheinz picked up a chair and stood with it raised above his head for some time, an eternity, according to one witness, then put the chair down and communicating no further sat in it, like a king, another witness said, until the police arrived and he was taken away.

SALESMAN

People like him. They trust him. Because his smile is endless. Because his good points are warm. Because his car is clean and he inside it is more clean. He has run no one down, not a single soul. He is unworthy of hell. He has been loved. Has been the one reason. And the third between. Has put his fist through a wall and touched the blue air outside. He knows refusal in its thousand voices. His life is not fog in a suitcase. He knows where he is at all times. He cannot be ambushed. He has a house and a wife and a child and they are entirely solid. And immovable. He is Trevor Beals and Trevor Beals has never not been Trevor Beals. Why do his shoes weigh a hundred pounds? Why does he dream of cow skulls? Whose tears are these? Why won't they stop?

SWEETHEARTS

He knew more than he said, laughed well, was an able dancer; there was a bar in the pool; he would never have problems; but Conrad was seventy and Margot was young. Still, they kept in touch. When Margot divorced, when she lost her job, when she felt light as a handkerchief and stepped off a balcony, it was Conrad who saw reason, Conrad who was kind, so when her father disowned her and Margot lived in her car and the worst moments of her existence kept repeating, it may have seemed natural to wind up where she did, because Conrad enjoyed feeding her and bathing her and cutting her hair and they could sit for hours in his basement without speaking, but sometimes Conrad forgot his better self and hated the hundred little things a woman needs and on those painful days he left Margot chained in the dark and turned up the stereo and floated in the pool until the unpardonable animal that had entered him consumed him, and spat him out, and they could start building their happiness again.

LEDGERMAN'S DILEMMA

Driving around in the killing heat, Saul Ledgerman discovered he could not, where he always could, take the sharp right to his office and climb the ziggurat of paper there, nor bear the sharper left to his house, where he was, despite himself, needed, only grip the wheel harder and try to ignore the fury in his heart, so long desired, now feared.

*

Spring hammered up, the air smelled of earth. Ledgerman surprised himself by going to a ball game, but there was no game. So he went to a movie, a foreign film about a gangland turf war. He identified with everyone.

Ledgerman was having a new suit fitted when he felt the lid on his skull lift and all his rare, improvident knowledge, in a stove's updraft, tumble lightly away.

Early one morning Ledgerman was laughing, because he often saw the humour where others didn't, in the height of the clouds and the wetness of the rain, and wondering where his shoes might be, and whose driveway was this, anyway, he was lying in?

A woman he had slept with, and twice represented in boundary disputes, didn't recognize him in an elevator. The foolish expression on his face was still with him the next day.

One of Ledgerman's clients, a psychiatrist accused of unlawful confinement, asked how he was feeling. Natural, said Ledgerman.

The way his wife and daughter, separately or in tandem, scraped any chair they sat in never bothered him before.

Ledgerman spent more time at the greyhound track, more time in the sloped room above his garage, batting a tennis ball against a wall. When he came out it was too soon to be black but there it was.

The curb is not a footstool, his father said, looking a long way down. Why can't he forget that?

Not far from his house a pier stabbed into the ocean. Ledgerman threw his phones from there.

*

Greyer, fatter, slower, Ledgerman woke up at the bottom of the night and went for a walk on an expensive beach. Nothing is lived down, he told the warm breeze. Endurance is the penance of the weak, he told the waves wetting his shoes. The sun would come looking in an hour, he told himself, in his kindest voice.

THE ENEMY KNOWS THE SYSTEM

Lloyd Powers, actuary, asphyxiophilist, diabetic, relaxed the red scarves and began his retreat from the day by counting the flies – thirty-eight alive – in the monkey palm, then pouring more bleach down the drains. It was probably November.

Lloyd has lived with himself for a long time and is prepared to continue. His supplies are adequate. He is not wasting away. He keeps dry clothes in every room. These are furnished rooms and Lloyd can defend them. He is sharp of mind. At any moment the full force of his attention can be turned to a single ramifying crack in the plaster. Or he can lie on the floor right now and separate this instant from that instant and take his sweet time not putting them back.

Lloyd has timed the startle reflex of rodents. Lloyd has seen the seven stars fall from the sky. The end of the world has come, come and gone. The sky is still there. Lloyd is still here.

Salvation is not for everyone.

FINE, DON'T MENTION IT

Yesterday, or the day before, Heather was down on her knees with her head in the oven when she smelled, of all things, Tim's foot powder. Later, she assumed it was later, she noticed Tim's place at the table, set. His special spoon. His deluxe salt shaker. When she called him, as she'd been meaning to, she didn't mention any of that. Or how, for some time now, a sort of sleep could drop her anywhere, in her chair, off a cliff. How she felt herself seen, by the eyes of a thief, each time she woke up. Tim had no interest in those types of things. So she told him she opened a window, to change the air, and a bird flew in. How it flung around like it owned the place. How she shut the window. How it snapped its loud neck. How she was wondering what in heaven, if he was there, they thought about that, if they thought at all, if it wasn't just motorsports and fried potatoes and chasing the cunt day and night, as he must have expected.

ACTOR

My character is tired of blame, but there it is, beating his eardrums. *I will squint into a constant sun.*

My character has not learned from his mistakes because he loves his mistakes and no one learns anything from love. *When I look at my hands I know they belong to someone else.*

My character is selfish and more intelligent than me. *Every third line, or fifth line, must be whispered.*

My character stands in doorways as if he owns their emptiness. *My smile swallows the camera.*

In the party scene my character is naked while clothed. *We are all zoo animals.*

In the sauna scene my character is clothed while naked. *I will pretend I am being interviewed.*

My character is dying and no one believes him. *I drop my wallet, I drop my keys, I drop my watch, only then do I collapse.*

My character feels darkness touch his face. *Just like Dad.*

TWENTY MINUTES

Dean Lawson was a man at sixteen, feared and respected, then a car battery exploded in his face. He became a roller in a steel mill, an electroplater, a boozer, the guy who took people's appliances when they couldn't pay. And met Juanita Paul. Her husband had just hanged himself and she was banging around in a bright void. Dean liked the little she had on at a party. He was renting an A-frame beside a motel then. It was like being a guest, he said. Except you don't have to leave.

A swimming pool at night can be the world's best place.

Juanita's court date was pushed back. Dean's moods evened out. They altered their tattoos. They made extravagant plans. Summer blazed into fall.

One morning Dean had some fentanyl to pick up. When he got back he found Juanita not breathing in the bathtub. She had known almost nothing about him. He could never have that again. The A-frame burned to the ground in twenty minutes. Dean watched it all the way.

SILENCE

After a lifetime of fear, Julius broke the funeral home window and climbed in. It was just as he remembered, one soulless living room repeated to eternity. There sits his father, smoking a cigar. There stands his mother, screaming with her mouth shut. Julius shows them the rock in his hand, but it is only his childish hand. His father reads the newspaper. His mother chews her hair. She chews her hair and vacuums the heavy carpet, the heavy drapes, his father's heavy thighs. Julius wills the ceiling down. His mother leaps out the window. His father crawls. His mother swans in a yellow dress. His father snaps his suspenders. The ashtrays multiply. The Christmas tree burns. His mother throws a glass. His father shatters. Julius runs. Somewhere a dog howls in the enormous night.

ALL THE LOVELY JUDIES

slant rain and the wind stiff, Jon Tropp was tramping the woods, a five-acre birch and alder stand out behind his house, he was hunting partridge but his mind wasn't on it and the ache in his hip began probing its needle so he thumbed the catch on the .22, whistled, and the dog emerged snuffling from a burdock thicket, snorted and shook and they started back through the cold slap rain and grasping mud

when they reached the house a squirrel caught Tropp's eye, a fat blacktail scamping the garage roof, he gauged the frolic, fired, scraped his boots on the step and went inside, into the kitchen, his kitchen now, plates stinking the sink and a mouse-trap sprung, he hung his jacket on the floor, poured a tumbler of whiskey, and spread the paper to the race news

two hours later Tropp was naked in the basement room he never went into, swinging a hatchet, swinging and cursing and chopping the mannequins, all the lovely judies Netta left, beating the hate out, then he sat on the sewing box and surveyed the destruction, twenty years worth, then he found a broom and swept it all up

Tropp believed in luck, just not for him, but that afternoon he was barrelling the truck through a thrash of rain, headed for the track, he had a feeling wouldn't leave him alone, an unknown pacer name of Lonely Woman going long odds in a claiming race, weather this rough she'd be looking to run, he'd learned that much, might as well make some damn money off it

SATELLITE

Late in their marriage, the Steinbachs, Phyllis and Lowell, planned a trip to New Mexico. They wanted to die happy, under adamant stars, in the atomic age. The convertible they leased was the light, optimistic blue called robin's egg. Phyllis spent several months matching her outfit to her sun bonnet. Lowell stayed in his pyjamas and arranged the blankets and golf balls they would need. When the day came that Phyllis died, after a brief humiliating illness, Lowell was living on the other side of the world, planning a trip to the moon.

SIXTEEN MOMENTS

Eamon Fell has a prescription to fill, an important drug, but is nowhere near a pharmacy when he remembers.

There is hardly any water in the culvert yet his shoes are wet through.

Why these scratches?

Days like this he should stay inside. That was usually the best answer.

Eamon sits on a bench and lets the sun swat down.

Butterflies are few in the Memorial Garden. No one else seems to notice.

Good morning, he says, as if it were up to him.

The carousel is not crowded.

The red are more nicked and faded than the gold horses.

Some of the children are quite beautiful.

Don't be afraid can be the wrong thing to say. He must have known that at one time.

In his room he can sing along with the radio and match the emotions put in front of him and not miss them when they are taken away.

He can put clean hands behind his head and have the feeling of strolling in a pine forest while lying on his back.

Misunderstanding follows him like a dog.

Eamon throws the little purse as far as he can.

UNHEIMLICH

When he was too old to be carried and too young to resist, Udo Gebhardt accompanied his mother on an endless walk along the Drei Brücken Kanal. Thirty years later he watched a seabird struggle in the gray wind and wrote *Memory is a cannibal*, crossed that out and wrote *Despair is a promiscuous god*, crossed that out, got himself dressed and went for a walk, a gray walk back and forth along the Drei Brücken Kanal, then returned to his hotel, removed his clothes and wrote into the night, crossing out nothing until the last anger abandoned him, and he began again, and wrote *Memory is a cannibal*.

The resulting brief book made Gebhardt's career, which was long and unhappy, in pediatric psychiatry.

TRESPASS

Having received from trusted sources information of a disturbing nature, it seemed to Hans Daimler only prudent that he monitor personally the vulnerable bounds of his property, and this he did, for three nights.

The first night, with tight steps, for the leaves were slippery, he advanced as far as memory allowed, and was relieved to find, intact, the bandstand shining in his slight beam. The air was too thick to see farther into the deer park of his youth, but that was to be expected, given the recent fires, and he was satisfied by the shadow of a leap.

The second night Hans slid back an enormous bolt and ventured to the lawn's horizon, where the spoor he followed became solid and familiar. Breasting brittle grass, he emerged at the boathouse. No fearful mists embraced him. The sole tracks were those of small creatures. He verified the respirations of a sail. He was glad to leave.

The third night, pushed along by a sorrowful breeze, Hans circled the orchard one hundred times, each time discovering that he wanted no more from the world than permission to stop, although he was not in the least tired. Eventually Hans called out, or was called to and tried to answer. In either case it was then that Dr. Himmeldorn, who two years previous in a transport of religious clarity had strangled The Adversary in the form of his wife, objected.

The struggle was mortal.

Humour and scrupulous hygiene had won the doctor many friends in the ward and these took his side vigorously at the inevitable inquiry.

OLD HER

Alice has her house, the porch out front, gazebo behind, the neighbour's dog who knows her. She has her bad sleep. And her hunger, a wild hunger with no sense of proportion. The more it eats, the more inside it wants. The hole in her good eye is one of its mouths now.

Alice puts a fresh coat of paint on her wedding shoes and goes out rain dancing. The garden wears its finest glister. When she falls, into glass hollyhocks, crashing the best of them down, down, down, it seems slow, and not wrong.

It was warm for February. Her little soul animals she did see frolic.

COAL TOWN, WINTER

You can't shoot rats at the dump anymore. Last year's jobs were better. Just three trucks outside the Legion. Miles of room at the church. The pawn shop stays open later. Sleet horizontal down Main Street. Electric heartbreak from the country bar. A fist goes looking for a brawl. Newlyweds return to the same apartment. Sky like an anvil. Deaf Bob moves in with the bootlegger's wife. The coroner checks the chains on his tires. Norm's daughter says the cancer had a life of its own. A certain slow thud that is sunset. Father Craig puts the razor to his wrist like a mother testing milk. A foot of snow climbs the helmets of the war memorial. An owl interrogates the night. Stop sign pocked with buckshot. Shush of a match in a can of beer. Everyone ages a little faster in the high school parking lot.

UNTIMELY

Nine months before his death, Sandor Gleason, bathing his broken foot, has the splash pad to himself. He weighs three hundred pounds. The sun is loud in his face.

Eleven months before his death, Sandor Gleason was supposed to meet Jake outside the Korean Barbecue, to explain and be forgiven.

Two years before his death, Sandor Gleason burned documents of world importance in a bathtub at the Wayfarer Motel.

Five years before his death, Sandor Gleason could find no reason not to hitch a ride out West – all he had to do was tie the man's arm and locate the vein.

Seven years before his death, Sandor Gleason felt strongly that he could stop his heart, with a single pointed thought, any time he liked, or let it prattle on mercilessly.

Nine years before his death, Sandor Gleason had *Caro*, in a jubilant blue cursive, tattooed on his chest as a birthday surprise for his wife.

Ten years before his death, Sandor Gleason looked out on the world from an office with clean carpets and air conditioning.

Twenty-two years before his death, Sandor Gleason played basketball, kept his marks up, and ran a trapline in the woods behind his cousin's farm.

Thirty years before his death, Sandor Gleason, goaded by friends, punched another boy in the stomach.

Thirty-eight years before his death, Sandor Royal Gleason, screaming, was baptized in the stone font of Our Lady of Peace.

II

CINEPHILIA

One slow day in a feudal century decimated by plague and famine a handsome young man buried his mother under stones and left the village of his birth to meet his fiancée – whom he had seen, ecstatically, but never touched – in the village of her birth, a forest away. Immediately the sun declared its weight and exhaustion put knots in Tomo's legs. Yet he reached the forest quickly, as if another man inside him had run all the way.

A path opened. Tomo followed it. The grass closed behind him. A bird screamed. A path opened. Tomo followed it. The grass closed behind him. A bird screamed. Again. Again. Tomo crawled under a tree. A white moon rolled in a black sky. It began to rain, a silver rain touching its way famously down through the leaves.

Before the first drops stained the young man's shirt and entered his dream – in which he will die, in his empty village, beside a pile of stones, in the embrace of a ghost – Vivian Samaroo, graduate student in comparative biology, took from her purse a single glove, of satin, slid the glove to her elbow and unzipped the pants of Victor Rieselbach, graduate student in linguistics. They did this, with variation, every Sunday afternoon, beneath the conjuring beam, for a black and white season of Japanese film.

Youth. Sunlight on flesh. Their small apartment. Noise in the street. Their small bed against the wall. Youth. Victor wears a white jacket, it is Vienna at night, he frowns. This woman's

31

drinks are expensive and she has no money. Only the ponds of her eyes, dark, pulling him down. Youth. He holds her feet in his hands. She adores his mouth. Youth. They live a floating life.

Then Vivian's illness progressed, surprising them both. Her wrists doubled in size; ulcers latticed her tongue. She had trouble walking, even with her cane. There were useless tears. Vivian's father arrived, from Trinidad. He looked at Victor, saw an unremarkable boy, said as much, apologized; embraced his daughter, cried, apologized; made arrangements for their flight. Victor could visit, when Vivian improved.

Victor finished his doctorate and took a position in Bergen – his stepmother was Norwegian, Wenke, an elegant woman. Victor's father, as good as dead after the second stroke, had his own room. As did Victor, for the first winter months. The father was cremated that spring. Victor stayed on. His career peaked, receded, found its destined level. Wenke turned seventy. Card games, dinner parties, an annual month in Spain – they enjoy their faithful life. When the new films come out, or the old ones come back, they often go. Wenke takes her cane, wears her gloves. They sit in the back row.

MINOT

Jan was making sandwiches in the kitchen, asparagus roll-ups, slicing the crusts with a dull knife. She would remember that. The twins were outside, playing in the long drifts. Pat was watching a football game with the sound off. Massive little men smashed around in snow.

Pat called her name. He didn't raise his voice. Jan sat on the couch beside him, up close where he wanted her, while he described, board by board it seemed, the ghost town he was building and how much better life would be when he was done and they could all move in. The reception was poor but he was confident she could see, if she made the effort, how well the crew was following his blueprints. Jan agreed. Pat released her wrist and ate the sandwiches.

She hid about the house whatever felt wise to hide until she ran out of places.

A week or some weeks later, it was hard to remember, Jan wiped or did not wipe the steak knife before she put it in her purse. It was a clear night nonetheless. The moon was right there at the door. She stepped on it going out, coming back in, going out again, a child at a time. She wasn't sure the car would start. She wasn't sure she could drive it far enough. There was this slow hypnosis of falling snow.

PORTRAIT

Young Francis fords a river, climbs a mountain, outruns a mad dog, finds a cave in the woods, learns to hunt without mercy, learns the punishment of fire, suffers the mystery of God's vast night and returns to the trailer park an hour late for supper, blistered to the elbows, dragging a kite.

Old Francis loses patience with his tablemates, their stink, their jut.

Young Francis meets a girl, Charmaine. Freckles begin at her shoulders. She can ease one heel behind her neck. They're driving, quarrelling in circles on a country road, and she leans over and kisses him and turns the ignition off. The steering wheel locks. She spends nine months in a cast. He's fine.

Middle Francis fails his accountancy exam the same week his daughter stops breathing in her crib. Bertilla can't sit still, or go outside, or touch him in any way. He can't hide his relief.

Old Francis makes a mask from a plastic bag. The eyeholes aren't right. Still, it's some protection.

Middle Francis sells half a million dollars of aluminum siding, has a pool put in, survives his first heart attack, buys a camper van, parks it in the driveway, sits out there some nights.

Young Francis puts a rifle barrel in his mouth to see what it's like.

Middle Francis writes *unavoidable thought patterns* on a memo pad, then *hazarding along*.

Old Francis hears his wives demand a glass of water. He looks in the closet. He looks under the bed. He roams a long hallway, knocking on doors.

Middle Francis sees his double on a black street, rattling the door of a massage parlour. Then again at the zoo, striding back and forth.

Young Francis hopes his cache of shames won't get much bigger.

DIAMOND GUARANTEE AND LIFETIME
OF VALUE PLAN

After Gary, after Lou, Rachael had a hard time finding her place in a populated world. Her problem was – she didn't know what her problem was, but she felt inside out and feared it was visible. Every day had a second day spinning and wobbling inside it. What would she do with another year? She had some money, not enough. She bought a dying car, filled it with groceries and drove toward the prospect of new thoughts.

In the desert the light was sharper than Rachael liked but the shadows made up for that. *A stone's love is for the ground,* she read in the bathroom of a gas station, lipsticked on glass. Wind, the entire month of April, sang of ether, sang of rue – the true voice of the desert.

It was good to stop listening.

It was good to be none of God's business anymore.

RESPECT

Sullen in Vilnius, angry in Minsk, a thread of nausea entwines Mikita Boyko's heart. He is twenty-seven. He used to follow the harvest. Now he cleans offices at night. His father thinks he is a rising criminal. He walks three miles to his room.

Dogs don't like him.

One woman he knows is a wilderness. Another bewilders him. He worries, he explains, he gets no further. If Mikita had a girlfriend he would pick up his clothes and open the window and put his Ruger American on the table for her to see. Then he would take her bowling and they would both drink too much and insult one another. Her friends would have better jobs and he would suffer their straight teeth. When she told him she needed money for an abortion he wouldn't believe her. When she cried and refused to stop he would recite, in a voice deformed by weariness, her flaws and shortcomings.

He is of the fallen. He will die alone.

It is almost dawn.

SUCCULENTS

Ames, thin, abrupt, feared for his stinging voice, was a teacher. Whelan, a round man with tattoos he couldn't reach, had, before his accident, pulled intricate animals from glass, and was now a janitor. It was Friday again and they were drinking in the furnace room, Dixie cups of rye.

Ames was in a good mood – a solution to his mother had emerged that didn't involve him – so when Whelan, who had passion for cacti, the stunted hairy ones in particular, started in on mealybugs and fungal rot, Ames leaned his head to the furnace and listened to the wind in there and didn't interrupt for a while.

Ever pick up hitchhikers? Usually Whelan felt his emotions slide from their hole well before they were on top of him. There was this one, Ames said. His smile, always awful, got worse. A dwarf almost. But the thighs on her! Could've crushed a horse.

Whelan, driving in the desert, as he often did after his accident, had met his wife that way, a small, savage woman who opened his eyes to the evil all around him, in the most delicate things, and got completely away with it. Ames could not have known. That didn't matter. His smile said it all. The nearest hard object was a can of floor wax. It did fine.

FORT! DA!

Elise Bonnaire was born into a silent house and so grew up unafraid of the canyons between people. Childhood contained but did not explain the thrill of theft nor the desire to be an animal, many animals, all at once, the kind that dig tunnels, that fly in the dark.

Her mother spent her better days in what was called the garden, ate very little, was prey to eschatological insomnias. Stop hissing, she said, to the porcelain cat. Her father was an important alchemist at the second-largest investment bank in Lyon, then Amsterdam.

At the metamorphic age of fourteen Elise was found in the company of a naked woman, then drove her mother's car into a light pole. The new school was wintery and dull. She learned German, she learned chess. Handfuls of pills helped. Gliding, flashing, she met an arborist, Jens, painting an X on an elm. She showed him the screws in her wrist, a rill of scar, the dark eye of the birthmark on her thigh.

When her parents died it was easier to be together. Elise went to live with her maternal uncle, as she knew she would. She had her own room, with a separate entrance. And her own money, which she spent on Jens. Quick, laughing, vivid Jens. He was connected to a commune in the Ardennes and when Elise thought she was pregnant it may have been there he vanished to.

Another person, Elise told her husband. They were drinking on a terrace in Toledo, exposed to the insistent sunset. It was their tenth anniversary. Life is irretrievable, Udo said. He understood. Udo understood everything. One of his patients, a girl of fourteen, had run a hose from a tailpipe into her parents' bedroom. Nothing human escaped him. If Elise put rat poison in his drink he would understand. It would be easy.

DOG DAYS

RESCUE

An era of confusion is a good time to meet.

Diane has small feet, large ears, a funny tipping-forward walk. I have large feet, small ears, a funny back-leaning walk. Less has been built on more.

Stealthing, spying, snapping flower heads – we get out. Do you know why squirrels scream? We do. And we agree.

Our neighbourhood – so wealthy – supplies event after event. Feral sprinkler hoses are exciting to stand on, for example. But can be treacherous. Like children – those children who offer ice cream and then just laugh.

Some days there are more hard than soft currents in the local air. And, yes, a rashness enters our relations – or simple malice – with others. Mail has been lit. Obscene declarations made, in luminous chalk, with big arrows.

I have tried, Diane has tried, we try no more. Our mistakes are poor teachers. If that makes some people uncomfortable, her husband can bury himself in the garden. See – plenty of room.

Diane and I, we have other, finer souls to dazzle. That elderly girl in the Tudor house, always at the window, could be, if she would stop frowning, one of those. Or someone who doesn't know us.

SISAL

Stinting, faulting, putting weights on everything in sight –
little death strokes add up, Diane – these days start moving and
then just lie there like that scratchy rug we don't get rid of.

Look, I want to say. There are the clouds. Here is the
ground. Nothing important has changed. Instead I think of a
marsh I was in once, which I enjoyed being in, and yet how
fetid after were all my steps. When I share this insight we are
both more lonely.

Thus we hunger. Thus we moan. And harbour – between
bitter and plain hardness, in that sweet spot – doubtful emotions. Long blue shadows, longer blue shadows – is this our
fate?

The wind is dark and old these days, this night. We do not
fear it well – only press our noses to the glass and watch the
lights across the way go nimbly out.

DELICIOUS

Yesterday, that hulking tome, who can lift it?

Not far, as the crow flies, is a hill we charge, for wild sky. The other side falls steeply in our spines. We didn't go. I don't know why. I smelled no rain. We stayed inside. We raddled, we muddled, we ran broken circles in tired light, and made again – of nothing rare – our own affray. Was that like listening – rush, lag beat, leap – to strife of mind itching to be nipped, nipped but not relieved? Oh, too much.

Sharp-edged thoughts picked up and dropped; Diane's skidding laugh begun in one room deadstopped in another; drinking, drinking, and still so thirsty – yes. But Diane's husband – we saw him first – didn't bother us. The house relaxed. Night came early. Delicious were the snacks we snuck.

FINALLY, SOMETIMES

If broody, sour, if smudged of soul, we are not by nature mean, but may be brittle and shatter into six or eight, even ten havoc pieces. This happens strolling, this happens not moving a muscle. This happens provoked by forces mysterious, like sirens, or Diane's husband. This happens waiting, by train tracks, in a plain hostility of daylight.

Sorting drear from dire, as it seems we must, is a hard puzzle. I fall asleep sometimes, other times retrieve Diane's inhaler and drop it at her feet, her tiny frantic feet, and retire to my personal meadow. Fat the butterflies, quiet the bright smells. I know who I am, where my body stops, where the world begins, how it grows because I let it.

Even so, I hear her thoughts, and the sound is many elbows in a small room, or a great stampede, and my meadow is ruined. I behead a blue flower anyway, but feel no joy.

And yet.

How easily this morning – we can't explain it – a three-note sparrow flute forgets us completely.

THE ABIDING SEA

Linda's father believes she could have left Ross, without a glance, but never the tall view from the verandah, the unlimited light always striking some part of their house.

Linda's sister believes a clear day will come, from a direction unseen, and erase all the false ones piling up.

Linda's mother believes every lawless thing she thinks of, then drops to her knees in the vegetable garden and begs God to stop tormenting her.

Ross has no beliefs at all. He drives to the firm, reviews contracts, reviews breaches, and drives home. The garage door stays broken. None of his clothes fit. He hates looking at the sea.

It has been six weeks.

Linda's friend, Arlene, pays Ross a visit. He doesn't let her in. She calls Linda's sister. They meet and are helpless together.

Linda's mother can't find a clean corner, can't stand the radio, fears the scorn in sunlight slamming off the sea.

Linda's father goes for walks on the beach – he didn't before. Or quarrel with his wife. Or split wood to exhaust himself. Or own a night-view rifle scope.

Security lights bang on and off.

Linda's father parks his car on the Shore Road and slides down the bank. Wind from the sea throws sand in his face. There will be, he concedes, another storm. But he will be the eye of it.

PRIME

Cowardice is no mystery. Everyone has their reason. Paul Blum found his in an apple orchard, breathing the sweet rot. He didn't have to be there. He just stopped his car and got out. No one chased him. He was not a boy beating his loud body through the high grass. He was forty years old, in the prime of life. He could think his own thoughts. Let the dark come on, and go home. His wife would recognize him. She always had. Let the dark come on, and not go home. Only follow the bed-spring sound of geese thrashing into the sun, like his father. The empty trees, the ground beneath his feet had no opinion. It was an endless evening in the prime of life. He could think his own thoughts.

LOVE AND STRIFE

Deaf to council, careless in delight, Shirley Dale, twenty-one, was popular at the hat factory.

Dennis Bunting, thirty-two, floor manager, wished to live apart from his companion, from the moment she moved in, he told Shirley.

Laureen Moore, thirty-five, receptionist, loved Dennis no less than ever and hoped that that was enough.

Dennis proposed to Shirley. Laureen became pregnant. Shirley took up with a lid press operator. Dennis fired them both. Laureen lost the baby. Dennis hired Shirley at better pay. Laureen spent too much time interpreting wallpaper. Dennis changed his cologne and bought a new car. Shirley saw a bright future wherever she looked. Happiness is not a crystal ball, Dennis told Laureen. Laureen thought the new car extremely red.

Time swung its axe.

Shirley found a problem in her breast. The factory failed. Dennis dropped dead in a dog park. Laureen moved into a bachelorette and sat there, surrounded by herself. As a child she reached out to people and tried to scratch their eyes – that kind of memory came back. She made a few odd calls after midnight. She understood her plants. Never had she known the sky so livid, so red.

REINHARDT

Reinhardt was born on the lost day of a leap year and by that reckoning was not yet ten. I'm the baldest boy alive, he said, not counting cancer. Across the restaurant table was a friendly woman. She laughed a little.

Laurie worked in a law office. Her earrings touched her shoulders. Her hair touched her breasts. Reinhardt sensed an ability to listen. He began a humorous story – about a priest, an atheist and a self-driving hearse – but he must have told it wrong.

Reinhardt works hard to tolerate. He takes the night shift, the balky forklift. He gets up early and runs terrible miles in any weather. If a car lost control and flew into a ditch, if a house blew up in front of him, he has no doubt, he would enter the fire, and haul the strangers out. In his apartment he can take off his clothes and stand in nature's light, the window well is that deep. Then his ex-wife calls and he feels no rage. Is that not enough?

Everyone punches a wall now and then. He should not be confused with criminals. It was obvious he was capable of goodness. A life could be made of that. He wouldn't need much.

DEATH IS NOT AN EVENT IN LIFE

Wishful, ebullient, innocent of doubt, the late David Ware, of the Baltimore Wares, had by his fourth decade buried enough marriages and survived enough lawsuits to realize that, in personal as in commercial life, whatever went bad got worse, often much worse, and not to view that as a serious objection, until, perhaps, one unnaturally lucid June midnight at The Pines when, mistiming a magic trick, he astounded his guests by dashing, ablaze, the length of his yacht and in a cough of steam disappearing beneath the inflexible placidity of the lake.

SLOPE ROAD, 1980

Burns Tapley wouldn't kill spiders, or any crawling thing in his house, only gather them into napkins and drop them outside. When a working man in good order he spliced cable on draglines, then ran the excavator until his nerves quit. A truck could have fit in the bucket easily. Before that he moved around a lot.

The place on Slope Road had four rooms and the whole woods behind. Burns didn't need more. Anyone who knew him would have said so. He hated the telephone, cut his own hair, owned a large globe he liked to spin and stick his thumb down on. He had a wife in Sudbury once. Nobody knew that. Their boy drowned. Sometimes he watched television, sometimes he couldn't stand it. Thursdays a local man with an honest voice had a Gospel program on the radio. Once or twice a week Burns drank himself carefully into a stupor and slept in his shoes. Sundays he picked wildflowers or baked a loaf of bread, maybe an apple pie, and walked a mile, although he owned a car, to the home of his friends, an elderly couple, for a hot supper.

Burns was forty-eight, then he was fifty-two.

One Monday the ironing board was tipped over and Burns found beside it, not a mark on his naked body. The house was neat, for a man's house, and somewhat clean. No pictures. A cold pot of oatmeal on the stove. A metal strongbox was discovered under the bed. They didn't have to force it. Inside were train tickets, unpunched, and a stack of letters, from a woman and to a woman, not the same woman, and one ear, dark, with an earring attached.

YAZAN

Waiting to be seen, for her head to stop bleeding, for God to like her, Amina Mansour, twenty-three, widow, discovered she could throw her voice, that stiff, shabby, featherless thing, and throw it far, down the white hallway and out of the clinic, into the tumult of Al-Jabr street, and on, through the burning dust, to the door of her house, where her house had been, and Yazan, who was proud of his garden, the tomatoes on the roof, the four impossible lemon trees, but not far enough, never, that it wouldn't fly back and tell her all about it.

THERAPY

He can feel himself slide off just walking along

When he has to write his name he makes a mess of it

A woman in the gym asked if he'd been in an accident and he said yes

He kills in his dreams and it's easy but Sean owes him money and he does nothing about it

Like a scarecrow nobody's scared of

His father can't look at him straight

His mother wants a piece of his day a small piece every day

He bought himself two prostitutes but they were both bad actors

The third was heavily pregnant

He wears a pair of socks once maybe twice that's it

He could drive a taxi to the end of his days and it would be the same night

Crack when opening crack when closing his tired mouth

Waking up in a basement was never his ambition

He could easily send away for one of those kits

The one thing he's proud of

The best parts of himself

As a kid he had steady nerves and good judgement

If his smile cohered

If he had throttle control

If his soul was not a palace of filth

He would see the same morning everyone saw

If he were someone else

LANDSCAPE

A white horse moves its bowels in a field of winter wheat. Dung steams to heaven. It is one kind of morning, and twenty below. Even the shadows are stiff. The dead man's brother throws stove ash on the snow. He will be late for the wake or simply not go. He would like to sit upright in a hard chair for the rest of his life. And watch unearthly silver birches split the dark, then that seep of blue.

Kitchen light, so early, is a flagrant thing. And austere. The way a brother hears the wind put its shoulder to the door. The way his wife for a week is nowhere. The way two black shapes, at opposing fence poles, emerge into crows and pick their way through a careless world.

MIDNATTSSOL

When Per Olsen, communications consultant, started the drive to Tromsø, for the hundredth time the drive to Tromsø, the irremissible light was level in his eyes and he was ready to marry Tiril Sandvik, ready to tell her so, as often as she needed. Tiril, tall, graceful, taught children to sit still. To raise their one hand. To cry and forget about it. She was a good person otherwise. Although unfaithful. Per was eleven years older. Tiril thought him a patient man, of deep understanding.

Crouched in the ancient darkness of his grandfather's barn Per once watched a kitten investigate a rat trap – it was something like that he felt on a straight stretch of road, halfway to Tromsø. It was midnight, it was morning, the same sun. The horizon was low. The light seemed to force it down. And melt the bones of his face. Per stopped. He had always feared the wrong things. Now he didn't have to. He got out and helped the young man as gently as he could into the ditch and retrieved the bicycle and dropped it over and stood in the road and let the sky interrogate him.

There was no real damage to the car. But he would buy Tiril a new bed. He would find some weakness in her and praise it. They would live more happily than many. Per got in, raised a hand to shield himself, and drove on.

CELIA IN THE EARLY MORNING

Age ten Celia Troy's ideal job was ambulance driver

Eventually she stopped cutting herself

When her mother died her father turned his face to the wall

Stepping out of girl into woman she liked her weak broody self
balled up & thrown

Celia's third boyfriend was a car thief the fifth loved any drug
he could get his hands on the eighth kept buying guitars & not
playing them kept slapping her leaving coming back the ninth
had no fear whatsoever Phil broke into houses & took what he
wanted he wanted her

They lived in a converted storeroom behind a barber shop the
customers were old Italian men with elegant manners Celia
worked in a cafeteria they bought a hotplate & a table &
pinned a poster over the bed a tropical waterfall Phil strung
lights in the yard oxycontin was their closest friend

In a year they were two phantoms trying to look solid

When Phil got out of prison Celia was pregnant

Who to remember who to forget she couldn't keep up

Phil went back to prison

Celia hated the clean women at social services

If she stripped the bed if she fed Gabriela's cat if she went down
the hall & started a conversation & carried it to its end &
didn't spill a drop maybe then

Pushing forward hanging back this rooftop feeling wouldn't
leave her alone

Her son learned to walk without her

WHEN I FELL FOR YOU

Kim Mack's last date wore a ball cap, indoors, for the glare. The one before was unpardonably grateful. She will be forty-eight in February. She's lost some weight.

The husband, a life ago, had a heart attack on the highway. It's her duty to say it, Hugh sees that plainly. Kim describes the dark time, her emergence. She hears her false notes. She is a strong woman, Hugh says. They order more wine.

Hugh Overton's wife left him for his cousin, second cousin, but still. He was angry all the time, and then, just like that, he wasn't. He's fifty, he says, a strange number to wake up to.

Hugh wears his clothes well. They seem to float. And Kim likes his house. It's set back from the road, a few trees. She has never been with a bald man.

They go biking, play some tennis, have sex in the car, like teenagers. Kim bakes a vegetarian lasagna, Hugh is proud of his omelettes. They visit Hugh's father, who is very deaf, who takes Kim's hands in his, whose ancient skin is a soft black leather. He says his son has done well, with his lovely wife.

Hugh's not a good swimmer, Kim is, they splash about in Burnt Head Lake. It's a place they like, discovered together, in these spacious days. Time rushes toward them, not away. Hugh stands on a sandbar. The water laps his chest. Everything is easy, everything fits. Kim dives between his legs, surfaces behind him, hangs her arms around his neck. The hot sky forgives, the hot sky forgets.

They could fall asleep like this. They could drift. They could vanish. They could wake up and find themselves lost, naked and abashed – in a year, years, in a scramble of months, some unbearable morning, whenever the blithe serpent of days might turn and betray them. They know this, of course they do. Kim kisses Hugh's back. Hugh shifts his feet and lifts her a little higher.

III

III

MIGRANTS

Moussa Fall smelled of stones. The gods he loved best were fresh fruit and television. He drank a little rum. He could cut your hair. A wild xalam almost put out his left eye. He had some trouble with his brothers. He carried his shadow on his back like a house. The laugh people remember is youthful. He left his footprints in the sea.

*

Omar Diagne had a cousin in Malaga, who had a friend in Ceuta. If he sold his tools and motorbike it was possible.

In another life he never gambles, he owns the repair shop and a house in Tambacounda, the entire top floor under the sky, he is married to Zenoba Touré, she stays beautiful, nothing can harm them, he grows wise, his sons and daughters are not seeds on the wind.

In this life he has to trust Souleymane.

*

In Bamako mistakes are serious. Yusif Diaw knew two men killed for gasoline. Another, younger than he, had to shoot his father. Courage is the law. His girlfriend is a Christian from Eritrea. His shoes embarrassed her at first. They are both bad dancers. She smiles when she's sad. Winta – her name fills his mouth. Only her hands understand him. And the dogs.

*

Sunglasses, cellphones, every kind of card, scuba gear, a Jeep, two Ivorian passports, a wedding ring, a box of Italian shirts – the best of Lamine is his thievery. He moves like smoke. The moon can't find him. He is nineteen. Or seventeen. His new last name went extinct in his pocket.

*

There is always less.

Abdul Wadood carved six years in a woodshop. Yet his hands are empty. And his eyes are worse. A headache can seize him, throw him to the ground. He tries to forget this. His daughter looks like her mother. He does nothing for them. In truth, they make him angry. He tries to forget this.

God asks too much. Abdul is twenty-five. Ducking hooks is the feeling.

*

Mamadou Kahlil Mbaye was born under blue tarp, fourth of five. His father was a miner in Burkina or the Hausa called Sampson who sold clean water. A lazy boy, said his mother, only games in his head. He sells watches in a market town. He grills kebabs and breathes bus exhaust. A few drops of battery acid change his fingertips. He is not too young. His prophet is the tallest of the dead.

*

The excessive sea never stops. Miles of wind put a fist in Ousmane Diop's back. At sixteen he hated the man in his mother's house, now he knows he's just like him, dogging his life waiting for luck. He'd rather climb a wire fence than sit on the ground forever. Rather chance the desert in a beat-up truck than the sun slap his face the same way every day. Same salt in his eyes, same sand in his heart. The empty sea never stops.

*

46 degrees – and this is morning. Bilal Deng drops his hoe and enters a vision of himself lying in a field, a different field under daytime stars, grass grows between his ribs, through his shirt to the strange sky, but he is not angry with the goats eating his magnificent grass, he is pleased.

McGINNIS

Duff McGinnis spoke with his son every week on the phone, and dreaded it, then every evening. He almost made a fool of himself in church, again in the grocery store. Deer got into the garden. Then McGinnis' wife, as expected, died. He was seventy-one and had always been where she was.

That winter he needed to build something. He converted Sarah's kiln to a steamer and fed it long strips of white ash. By spring he had given away a dozen toboggans. He could do the same next year. He could be that person.

There are times he can shut his eyes and see anything he needs to see. There are times he doesn't belong in his life and a truckload of white ash is a terrible commitment.

He would like to be grateful. He would like to break something precious. He would like to have no more to do with fitting the days together.

REVANCHE

Mr. David and Mrs. Dahl, by separate means, arrived at the hotel almost simultaneously. The pretence was a pianist once scandalous, now merely eminent. This is the last, says Mrs. Dahl. Again she is not believed. They spend an hour in their room. The feeling is thin as silk between them. Again he seems to know her, yet admire everything about her. They get dressed, find a bar. The waitress is young, soft, like a lamb. Mrs. Dahl imagines Mr. David making love to her, bending her, breaking her down. Night falls. They make the necessary calls and try to lie quietly. They listen to the rain repeat in the courtyard, a tired rain. The moment grows. Mr. David has never been more handsome, more banal.

DELAWARE

Clayton Rush was inside his new history and not looking out when he met Penny Tranh, in a geodesic dome, as it happened. No voice is the same as another, he said, tonguing her navel, but who recognizes their own? Neither had mushroomed before.

That night, and throughout their ardent journey toward Delaware, Penny told Clayton fables of her life, some of them true, and Clayton told Penny no, he had not always shaved his head, yes, he could eat the same thing every day, and maybe he had broken a bottle and rolled in the glass a time or two but he wasn't tempted now.

Clayton's truck had a crew cab and a blanket, he might have lived in Baja, might have been some kind of cowboy, he could tie and untie a slipknot with one hand, siphon gas in broad daylight, his credit cards had different names, he smelled good, his skin held extra heat, and Penny had seen his soul, it was the same size as her own, but not ugly, she could live with it.

Maybe the weather, maybe the acoustics of the turnpike – there came a sullen café. They were both exhausted. There was no pie. Absurdly, as if forced on them, a quarrel began, and grew, and ruined the privacy between them. That's the way witness protection works, Clayton said at last. It was the first time he was unconvincing. Penny had the strong urge to scratch his face.

Penny went out to the truck and retrieved her bag. Clayton didn't follow. She took off her slippers, put on hiking boots, picked up a large rock, smashed the passenger side window, dropped the rock on the seat and started walking.

At a campsite Penny phoned her husband. The year was not up, nowhere near. Matthew was still heavily, proudly involved with his neurologist, his psychiatrist, still injecting himself, still suffering, complaining, absorbing everyone around him – Penny could not imagine him otherwise. They agreed to meet, as soon as he was free, in Delaware.

TELEOLOGY

Gerald Betts had just thrown a hunting knife into the ceiling of his apartment and assumed below it the necessary posture when he was awakened by a series of sharp knocks. Naked, he opened the door. Sorry to bother you, Reverend, said the woman he knew as Ruth or Lorna, but my sister can't breathe.

Twenty years later, on the eve of his execution, Gerry Best received a telegram. Better days ahead. Yours in Christ, Lauren. Gerry's first thought was that one of the women he had killed was taunting him. He searched, yet his memory had never been good, and was now terrible.

Fatso was strapping his ankles to the gurney when, fondly, the fishbone came to him.

EVERYTHING LOOKS FINE AT THE END
OF THE STREET

When Hall de Groot was eight or nine, his mother, at the wrong time of day, ran his bath, and did not forget the bubbles, as she often did, but he was too big to drown. Hall's wife, so much younger, asks him why he's laughing. I'm too big, he says. She tells him he is the same as always and soaps his back.

Hall has been to the store already, and will go again, although it is Sunday and the store is closed. Until then his lawn chair is well-positioned, for his strong interest in the differences of shade. The brim of his cap. A caterpillar discovering sunlight.

Hall's favourite son doesn't love him. It's like two dogs, he tells himself, then is not sure how, is not sure why. He tries again. It is like two dogs.

But Hall's new wife is certainly much better. He is not afraid to say so. The other one couldn't keep her clothes on in company. He was not afraid to say so. If she were alive Nancy would return his calls, in the middle of the night, and describe her body, and criticize him.

Recently Hall watched a documentary on his giant television. It was about a man who spent nineteen years in a coma, and emerged, and went blind watching television. No, said Hall, he just pulled the forget switch. You can see it in his eyes.

Hall's teeth are bad but his smile belongs to a good man. His preferred flannel shirt retains its sharp colours. He is recognizable. The people in the store are glad to see him. His wife is glad to see him. No one flees. He is not lied to endlessly. His wrist is healing nicely.

The end of Hall's street is higher than the beginning. He has been an engineer, he can calculate slope. When the rain is heavy a dark flood hurries past him. He will watch it closely, for as long as allowed. Never yet has it wiped the earth clean.

CISTERCIAN

Having pledged no further harm, Elias Wye, forty-four, dying of lung cancer, conjured in his cell a six-foot wind harp which, blown on, returned him to his father's house. The massive door was locked. Elias called out. It began to rain. Elias heard his voice tear into pieces. He bloodied his hands. It was too cold to weep. He walked to the river. He had fished there often, but never swum. The rain made the water black.

What is love but fire? What is sin but rust? Everything solid is cruel in the light. It is time to get up. His brothers are waiting. They are good. They will cherish him. They have no choice. He has only to ask.

ALL HALLOWS

As the years piled up, Bruce Rutledge, like many criminals, came to appreciate straight dealing and peace of mind. His wife and ex-wife were friendly, two of three sons were employed, the mortgages were paid; his most recent court appearance was nine years ago, as a character witness. At fifty-five Bruce knew when to let things go, when to bear down. He had that reputation. The heart attack, it was true, had humbled him some, in his private hours, but the best vision he had of himself, thrown into the future, seemed undiminished, if not thrown too far.

Bruce was getting brake work done on one of his tow trucks when a call came on the burner phone. That's too bad, he said. And it was. Gord Rempel had been a likeable guy. As far as Bruce knew, no one harboured anything serious against him. He must have made a mistake.

Bruce turned off the highway and took the old road to Sharp's Mountain. It was autumn, the late edge of the season, and he enjoyed the ignited red uprush of the trees, the harmless gold torches. The car he was hauling was a simple accident, nothing memorable. It had been ready in the barn at Albert's when he got there. Bruce let himself in. The barn was cool, quiet, a place out of time. As he drove away Bruce saw Albert's wife on the porch, taping a witch to the door. They waved.

Vincent swung the gate and Bruce drove in and backed up to the crusher. In a better world Rempel's sin, whatever it was, might have weighed differently, but who lives there? It didn't bear thinking about for long. Bruce had candy to pick up and a pumpkin to carve.

GLOVE

Levi was kidnapped by wolves, to raise as their own. Alf rescued him. Alf was lost in the Arctic, tottering, delirious. Levi rescued him. They were new friends, the same age, Levi the larger, Alf the faster. It was a boundless Saturday and they had the field to themselves, the pricking cold, the long wind, the frozen cattails to battle with on the runoff pond. They could see Alf's house from where they were on the ice.

Alf's brother, sick with the flu, was playing games on his computer. His mother was making soup.

The big hole was round, in the centre of the pond, like the dark pupil of an eye. The small hole near the bank had no definite shape. The wind slid a glove about.

TRUST

Cal Bender didn't trust banks. When his wife died – high school reunion, heat stroke – he stopped farming, sold the land the new highway went through and began his singular life as a rich man. He bought a shining truck he didn't need and put a quarter million miles on it.

He liked country music, baseball on the radio, Friday night Bingo, Saturday Bingo. Some people assumed he was lonely. He didn't drink. Wouldn't paint his house, for tax reasons. There was a female friend, then there wasn't. Sometimes he thought he had put the world to sleep.

Cal's daughter was a sorrow to him, a spontaneous child who never grew up. There were too many drugs to play with. Life ran ahead and hauled her along. Cal looked for his fault but couldn't find it. She lived in a trailer park. Cal paid the pad fee. Her new boyfriend was half her age. He's not a bad man, she told him, and seemed to believe it. They broke into cars was the word around town. He didn't see her much now.

One Friday night the back door opened. There were two of them but Cal still had the sense of himself as a capable man. The money was in the freezer, under the moose meat. By the time he would have told them his arm was broken and his mouth was taped and they had gone to look for themselves. Cal didn't hear much of that. They had also taped his nose.

Richard Allan Black was arrested the following Monday, without incident, at the residence of Cynthia Anne Brawley (née Bender). It was Christmas Eve day. They had already opened many presents. Cynthia followed in another vehicle, her father's truck, and was herself charged, with break and enter, willful confinement, theft of goods valued at less than five thousand dollars, and murder in the second degree, later that afternoon.

MOTHER

Is that a stye?

The world's full of orphans, Sweetie, some of them get along fine.

Yes, yes, I'm calling the ambulance.

Well, you're *not* a goldfish.

If you hold your breath long enough you'll see Grandma.

Why does your invisible friend need a knife?

Shush, everyone else is happy.

I thought you were the smart one.

LAUNDRY

Last week I told someone I was from Flagstaff, which is odd, because it's true.

Usually I just grab whatever and go, but there I was, folding, sniffing, folding some more, pretending I belonged.

Then this man – I'll call him Bill – strolled in. He had high white eyebrows and his fly was very open. Stuck? I said. And Bill said, How did you get here?

Well.

Apparently the worst car crash Bill ever saw, or ever hoped to see, happened in my birth town. The sun was in his eyes but he described it thoroughly, with blasts of air and ferocious gestures. Not everyone died, though.

You can't win them all, I said.

Bill took a funny step.

As a rule it's hard to know what old people feel, on account of the lag time. Not with Bill. I could tell right away a hard little mystery lived inside him, at the bottom, that was painful to reach for.

I said what I knew – when things went tragic the devil was in the details and he could quote me on that.

Those sitting falls, like a settling, that children learn to do? No. Bill fell off a building at my naked feet.

Yes, I gave him a nudge.

And I looked into his eyes. They were small and calm and I tried to imagine their unique perspective, thinking it might help me later on.

Instead I remembered my grandmother's farm, the smell of hot dirt and a thin, dusty chicken I was fond of, whose neck got wrung, but that was stupid, because Bill wasn't making that sound.

And I wasn't listening. I was telling him about my life in the desert. The fearful mornings, the wasted afternoons, the elating, erasing nights. That I could never go back. That I would spend my life wandering, lying my head off and wearing other people's clothes.

Bill accepted every word I said. We left it at that.

SIDEWAYS IN MEXICO

The last time H. woke up beside his wife she was gone and he brought her back and everything was all right for a while.

N. weighed ninety pounds. H. could pick her up easily, throw her across the room if he wanted. Or put her on his back and start walking. Instead he keeps a mirror in his pocket, to catch her breath.

H. sat on the edge of the bed and watched a fly clamber about on a piece of fruit. He had never seen one so bloated, like a human eye. When he touched it with his cigarette it exploded into a helix of smoke and he was amazed how long it hung there.

A picture in his head shows an outburst of rain. A tree overhangs them. He has no beard. N. is clean. In the cloche of that instant they are laughing.

Another picture shows the lamp black, ivory black, blue black of the cool night sky so close there on the rooftop they can drink it.

Not this open kiln, this white dust, the endless noon.

Not this clarity, as though gazing through a loupe.

Not this brutal face burying hers.

H. went for more walks by himself and let the dry winds blow his feelings around. Often he ended up in the market and wandered among the stalls. He liked the bright fruit especially but anything could be found there.

The pistol had no weight at all. Left alone it might have floated away. The second shot chased the echo of the first.

TOGETHER

What eludes, they have learned to agree, matters less than what endures. They were together when the wolf winds blew and shook the house and a great sadness devoured Anders and there was no floor where Ingmar stood, together when they stopped reading palms, when they lied, when they flinched, together when the nights fell apart and each lost in his own way the compass of the other's voice, and are together still, some days fearful, some days cruel, some days surprised at the absence of bars.

STIGMA

The location was prime, a mature lot on a cul-de-sac. The bungalow itself seemed cheerful from the street. A nice job had been done with the garage. Björn Demming was pleased. He checked his messages, made a call about another property, and went inside.

*

They liked to smoke weed and gamble on their phones.

He had abrupt places of tenderness he could show.

She was the first woman he didn't need to see through.

He was her fourth man.

They got a dog but there was something wrong with it. Then a parrot but there was something wrong with it.

What's a good day? Nothing too heavy falls on your head. She knew what he meant.

Someone called and she heard his natural laugh, open and sweet.

They didn't go to movies anymore, or restaurants, or the houses of friends.

He did the shopping mostly, then always.

The soul, he told her, escapes through the mouth. She should learn to be quiet.

He held her hand on the barbecue.

She never managed to hate him.

He bought bags of concrete and worked late in the garage, tearing the floor up, putting it back.

For six months he was afraid to leave the house, afraid to stay, afraid to eat, take a shower, close a door, afraid to speak.

He went out in a snowstorm. It was another planet. He walked to the hospital, stood across the road and tried to see in, then continued on to the police station.

*

The carpet looked new in places, worn through in others. In the master a crack in the window allowed a bloom of frost. Still that off smell in the wallpaper, if you got in close. Otherwise not awful, for the price. A little sunlight, a little paint. The right people will love it. Björn hammered his sign in.

IN VIVO

Leland Murray, of Laughlin, Martin and Murray, personal injury specialists, poured and drank another glass of wine, rolled to the living room, settled himself, stretched a pair of sheer panties over his head and opened a file on his computer. It was the apartment on Tyler Avenue, early in the marriage. Nicole's hair was her natural brown, and long, chopped the rough way he liked. She wore sneakers. Her right front tooth was still chipped. The man might have been Leland, only circumcised, and the voice young. He turned the sound off.

In another life, Leland, unbidden, attended a party, for his daughter's ninth birthday, held at his wife's house, which he considered his house, and there, after several small quarrels, played Blind Man's Buff with such vigour he was soon, crashing and bellowing, left alone, then asked to leave, then lifted and thrown into the pool. His neck struck the diving board.

Soft extortion settles most claims. When court is necessary Leland wears white, head to toe, and a wide red tie. He is Bandage and Wound. The wheelchair is a throne of a kind. Indeed, Leland has made progress. Toward what? The future, his physiatrist, psychiatrist, and housekeeper say. The Partners concur. Leland is forty-eight. He sees himself, at fifty, even sixty, through scratched glass, thickened, sloppy, making progress. Life swallows him whole. He doesn't feel it. He makes progress.

There is a haze of motes. Leland stands by the pool house. Nicole floats on her back. The sun dazzles. Ellie plays with her dolls on the diving board, throwing them in, fishing them out. Everyone is safe, everyone is harmless. Nicole smiles and waves. Leland zooms in. He will never see enough.

WILD

It surfaced in the boathouse, where they had gone to smoke and stayed to drink, that Jim's husband Monty Nayle, the noted bassoonist, had not, this Friday past, dropped in on his daughter and spent the afternoon looking at slides of Honolulu and playing with the baby. Rather, he drove to Moore's Point, to the home of Eli Random, the noted violist.

The marriage was young, still growing. There was room for error. Well before dawn everything was resolved.

Jim took Monty's car and went to an offtrack betting parlour, ordered two breakfasts and lost twenty-four thousand dollars. Then he found a mirror and combed his long hair. He had blood on his shoes.

VJEČAN

Leaves are falling, flying and falling. Faris, tired of autumns, leans on his rake. The sky in his chest hurts. He is only forty. The sun hides and jumps out, hides and jumps out. He would like to lie down. Leaves are falling, flying. No one will mind. The wind turns and a breath of burning passes through the yard. Irfan says goodbye and puts on his hat. Esma does not finish her knitting. Someone shouts like a slap. Asim falls in the mud. Who will feed the chickens? Who will bring in the eggs and not break them? The cobbler is crying. Faris walks in a line that is its own horizon. His father is tall beside him. They have nothing to say and it is better that way. The cobbler is crying and his nose is bleeding. Faris keeps turning around. The sky is too small to swallow the smoke. Mother is safe in the cemetery. They take the woodsmen's path, yes, somewhat like cattle. Then the forest is cold. Has it ever been colder? Only in winter. But birds are incessant in every tree. Black birds, black cries, he has never heard so many. Then there are no birds, only breath and feet, breath and feet, no birds in the world. Comes a turn, comes a rise. His father's hand finds his shoulder. Faris flies into a ditch. No one sees. He drowns in leaves. No one minds. The sky climbs down and sits on his head. For thirty years. He is tired. The sun hides.

WOLF HOUR

Anita Pelletier's new eye keeps her up at night. Drops of cannabis help. She wouldn't sleep much anyway. Television pours its blue. The furnace coughs. Separate slabs of darkness move.

Tomorrow she will wear the blouse that doesn't hurt and sit outside in the durable light of July. She will smoke her five cigarettes. The neighbour's cat will try to hide itself from birds. Brother-in-law Phil will come by and leave a few dollars for the turkey fryer, the electric griddle, neither used. Or brother-in-law Phil will have something better to do. She will watch the traffic and count the red cars, the black, the white. She will call her sister and not mention Phil. She will call the home nurse. No, she will call her son and leave a cheerful message. She will eat the tomorrow salad. What fucking else?

Anita could break a knee on the way to the bathroom. It's like paper cuts in her lungs. There are nights she would like three years, even one. There are nights, the same nights, she doesn't want the bother. She still regrets not marrying Dane Johnson, not standing up sooner to Paul. Her son will always resent her. Her sister will never not glide through life.

Tomorrow Anita will call the doctor and tell his receptionist that a mistake has been made, that the eye is too small, that the eye is cold, that an eye so small and cold cannot ever be hers. Better the hole.

KAIROS

Drums, tennis, languages – whatever Lee Christian liked came easily. In high school he wrote credible lines of poetry, surfed a little, had a German girlfriend, a professor's daughter. His own father was a doctor, of internal medicine, who enjoyed encyclopedias and water clocks. His mother was an alcoholic who left and came back, a few times a year. Lee was their only child. He had a talent to charm.

Mathematics to music, music to literature, a faint smell of decay followed Lee through several universities. Supervisors found his work radical, promising, undisciplined, ill-conceived, delayed, absent. In a high feminine voice his father mimicked whatever he said, whatever he thought, one violent dream after another. He published a single paper, on jokes and torture in medieval drama.

Lee was thirty. His scholarships ran out. The nurse he was living with gave him sixty dollars a week, then a hundred, then he rifled her purse. He developed a rough laugh, felt scratchy half the day. He fell in the street. Another night he keyed the wrong car and lost a fight badly. He started stealing lawn ornaments, breaking into sheds, turning a few simple tricks in the park. He invented a sister, Joy, and went door to door – bus fare to the funeral.

Standing in line, Lee met a woman outside a methadone clinic. They had a bill collector in common. Denna saw a better man unfinished. Lee saw a future to which he was not invited. For a good year they were always breaking up, which suited them, then Denna needed help, real help, not his kind. Lee tried to kill himself, but not hard enough. There was a lot he didn't remember.

Lee cleaned up a bit, enough to get, and retain, a job digging ponds, trimming expensive grass. It was something. He found a room. A church nearby gave out meals. He didn't have to pray, but he did. Some of the guys were friendly. He called his parents, the first time in years, and regretted it. He still felt stared at. He would never be free of drugs. He had no wishes larger than the day he was in.

Lee was in the parking lot of a mini-mall, having a smoke, drinking a coffee. A car pulled up to a gas pump and a man got out. He lifted the nozzle and stood with it in his hand. A woman was in the car. The man said something to her, or toward her, and put the nozzle back, and collapsed. Lee dropped his cigarette, stepped on it, and walked over. In five essential minutes he redeemed his life. Now it could go on without him.

Keith Hazzard writes stories, poems, and plays. As Jesus Hardwell he published *Easy Living*, a collection of short stories, with Exile Editions in 2011; the title story from that book appeared in *EXILE Quarterly*, as well as being included in that year's *Journey Prize Anthology*; another of its stories won a Silver National Magazine Award.

Keith's plays have been produced in Saint John, Guelph, and Kitchener.

He lives in Guelph, Ontario.

Photograph of author © Karen Smythe